Sister Faith's Diaries Volume 1

Life after death…

Cayonna Prince

ISBN-10: 1727026438
ISBN-13: 978-1727020436

DEDICATION

Sister Faith's Diaries, are dedicated to everyone with questions on how to serve the Lord. May these writings be a vehicle to bring you to a closer relationship with the Lord? These volumes are written for your entertainment and to spark conversation and research. The author in no way bases these writing to the total true gospel of the Lord Jesus Christ. If you find a nugget save it for yourself in a time of need or share it with someone you love.

Contents

Life After Death Party

???? - October 18, 2018

Sister Faith F. Christian

Order of Service

Prayer & Praise

Presentation of Life

Intermission

The Eulogy

Closing Remarks & Prayer

ACKNOWLEDGMENTS

Prayerfully these volumes become a platform to spark conversations amongst believers and not-yet believers of all ages.

When that happens I will be able to acknowledge the many people who inspire me to write. So, if you want to see your name in the acknowledgments; keep purchasing, reading and talking about Sister Faith and her diaries.

With that said, please don't measure your importance based on which volume you are acknowledged in. I love and need every bit of inspiration everyone sends my way.

Sister Faith's Diaries Volume One, I would like to acknowledge Pastor Myron McClain and Anthony Prince.

Anthony Prince, my husband. Thank you Anthony, for your honesty. You have shown me that it is a good thing to be the me who God created. Even when I think I am way off the mark, you find ways to show me I am still in the race. Thank you for being my partner in life and my support. I love you with that unconditional type of love.

Carrie Holland, thank you for being my number one fan. Your support and encouragement keeps things moving when I try to park.

I would like to acknowledge My Pastor, Myron E. McClain Sr of Labourers for Jesus Church and Ministries in Baltimore, Maryland The Original character for Sister Faith was conceived 2008 in the LFJC Drama Ministry. Thank you for arranging a platform for the gift of creativity to flow through my life. I never thought it would end up between the covers of books, but here we go!

HERE GOES EVERYTHING

I can't believe this service is where I am supposed to officiate for the first time in my life. The entire football stadium was filled and there were thousands of people flooding the parking lot and surrounding areas.

Who was this woman really? I have only known her for three months and I get a letter with specific instructions on how to officiate this service."

"Shake it off"!

Is what I tried to tell myself over and over again. Sister Faith, what in the world did you get me into?

"WWSFD? What would Sister Faith do? Pray!"

"Lord, please be with me as I stand before all these people and attempt to speak about your special servant Sister Faith. Lord, please allow me to complete the task before me while giving You all the honor and all the praises You are due." "Lord, while I have your attention and if it's not asking too much; and if it's not too late; could you please take this cup from me? Lord I am really not thirsty right now. Plus I think my cup is already running over. I'm serious Lord…I am praying these prayers in your name, Amen."

"There you have it, my every thought as I walked to the podium to stand before thousands of people and do the unthinkable. My task is to keep order for the most controversial woman I have ever met, this is going to be interesting."

"My heart was racing, it felt like it was about to jump right out of my dress and make a field-goal from the fifty yard line, where the podium was placed on a high golden platform."

Going out in style is an understatement. Sister Faith was a fireball full of life and this service was like nothing I had ever seen or even heard about in my lifetime.

"Here goes everything…" the music from a one-hundred man orchestra started to fill the stadium. Two-hundred choir members dressed in all white began to sing as they made there way to the stage.

"You can do this was the last complete thought I remembered. "

"Good evening and welcome to the Life After Death Party for: Sister Faith F. Christian," is what my instructions said to say word for word. After a ten-second pause I realized all these people where looking at me for direction and I had not one clue of what to say next. My instructions said loosen up and just talk, they are only people.

So I started by telling how I met Sister Faith. "Let me tell you a little history before we proceed. I met Sister Faith about three months ago at the mall. I was looking in the lingerie section looking for something special if you know what I mean. When this beautiful woman walks right up to me and says," "If he is not your husband he don't deserve to see you in that".

"At first I was upset. I thought to myself…of course… who in the hell is this woman all up in my business". "I know you cute and all old lady but you need to get all the way out of my business". But my mouth said,"excuse me ma'am, are you speaking to me?"

"I'm glad you asked," she replied with the biggest brightest smile I had ever seen. I started watching my surroundings incase she was the front man for some type of scheme, use the nice old lady to distract me.

It was my 13 year anniversary with my boyfriend Joshua. He had been my boyfriend since I was 11 years old. I thought I would spend forever with him, until I met Sister Faith.

She told me not to be alarmed, she was a servant passing through and I was her mission for the day. I laughed so hard when she said that, because I finally figured out what was happening. The church people are on the loose in the mall again, messing with people while they shop and mind their own business.

"Sorry ma'am, I don't mean to be rude but I am really in a hurry." Is what I said as I hurried to the counter to pay for what I tried to keep as my secret purchase. We see how that turned out, miss church momma all in my bags.

I left the store with my items and walked to the food court to grab a bite to eat. Low and behold who was already standing in line two people in front of me, none other than Sister Faith.

I thought how in the hell did this old lady beat me down the stairs. Just as I was about to go to another food station, she turned around and said,"please, do not leave on my account, come up here with me and let me buy your lunch". As I made my way towards this lady I thought,"what am I doing?".

I spent the next three hours listening to this stranger tell me my life story from the beginning to that very moment.

Not only did I have lunch with her that day, she has been a part of my life everyday until she departed this earth. I thought I would not make it without her. She has become my mentor, my minister and my friend.

Since meeting her and spending time with her I learned to see more of God in my world. Don't get me wrong I do not in any way profess to know how to live for God, I am trying everyday. So tell your preacher friends to back up and give me space to learn. When I said that the entire place erupted with laughter. I guess that was a good one.

Now that she is gone I don't know where to start my own walk with the Lord, but I will tell you this, I know I will reach my destination. I don't know how or when but I am going to reach it. The crowd let out a resounding applause.

I had to continue. "Three days ago I received a letter from Sister Faith and I would like to share it with you all today." The letter read:

Dear Stacy,

If you are reading this letter that means I am dead. Sorry to be so straight but hopefully you have been with me long enough to know, there is no need to beat around bushes unless you looking for WE EVIL. (weevil child, look it up) lol.

I am gone to a better place but you my dear are just getting started. God is pleased with the decisions you have made in preparation for your new walk.

Just don't forget to share your story, tell your testimony and never shy away from completing every mission the Lord sends you on. No matter who the message is delivered to.

Trust me He will be sure you are ready every time. Make sure your response at the end of everyday is mission complete boss! Seriously Stacy, you are special to the Lord and He wants to use you. Even when it hurts, let Him use you. While you're crying, let Him use you. Even when they say,"you must be crazy, let Him use you! When they didn't hear what He told you to do, let Him use you!

Stacy, never stop allowing Him to use you and life will be a wonderful adventure filled with new places, new people and most of all spreading God's Love. You got this baby-girl!

Forever Love
Sister Faith

I can't tell you why I read this letter to all of you, but it felt right. I am in no ways sure if I am doing this correctly but, let's begin with a word of prayer. Please humble your hearts.

"Lord, we are gathered here for the life after death celebration of your daughter Sister Faith Christian.

Lord join us in this celebration… as a matter of fact, Lord lead us in this celebration.

Lord speak to everyone here today. Lord show up and show us why we had the chance to know Sister Faith.

Lord we understand she is in the best place with you. If these people around me today knew her like I knew her, give all us the strength to live for you without her check-ins.

Lord set the atmosphere for this evening and may all of us yield to your presents. Let every mouth speak honestly today because Sister Faith was as honest as you make them, in the name of our Lord, amen."

Once I said amen, on key the orchestra and choir began to magnify the stadium with heavenly songs of praise.

Everyone in attendance was in personal praise. The praise dancers were dressed in all white flowing dresses with gold and purple ribbon flowing from their wrists. The orchestra, choir and praise dancers set an atmosphere of total praise.

The praise quickly turned into a worship experience like none I have ever seen. Every person was in his/her own place of worship. As I opened my eyes to see the seen before me, I thought, "this must be what heaven is like".

Worry began to set in. How was I gonna stop this worship to move the service forward? I had nothing to worry about, Sister Faith had already taken care of that.

After the third song, the praise dancers exited the field. After song four the choir disappeared from site but the voices were still singing strong. When we reached the fifth song, the orchestra began to dismantle right before us, leaving one drum and one saxophone player on the field. The choirs tone was now a quiet hum, while the drum and saxophone players played "Speak Lord".

Everyone took their seats and sat attentively as

the musicians ministered with their instruments. I had no idea how I was going to speak after an experience like this. These people are ready to hear from God, not me.

I always wondered how preachers can get up and talk when the place is so filled with the Spirit like this. There was no time to waste I had to keep the schedule, WWSFD? She would say, Just Do It! So I did. I stood in front of the mic and when I opened my mouth the words to the song that was playing began to flow from me. Those words came from a place I had no idea I owned.

When I reached the end of the song I realized the musicians were no longer playing and the field was empty. I was standing before all of thee strangers singing like I have never sang before. It felt like I was standing before God and I had to empty every bit of my praise because I may never get to this place again.

When it was over I said please turn your attention to the monitors placed around the field, stepped away from the mic and watched the presentation with everyone else. I thought,"wow, being a preacher is amazing. You get to visit God every-time you stand at the mic." With that exhilarating revelation the presentation began to play.

THE PRESENTATION

The voice of Sister Faith echoed throughout the stadium. "Hello from beyond!". Only Sister Faith would do something of this magnitude. A picture slide-show began to play on the screens. Pictures of churches, groups, preachers and children flooded the eyes of everyone in attendance. People began to see pictures of themselves and their ministries. After the slide-show, Sister Faith appeared on the screen, live and in living color. It felt so real like she was right there with us and still alive.

"Welcome to my Life After Death Party, that's right I said party. Now I know some of you uptight leaders will be offended by something said or done today. Guess what? I didn't care when I was there and I am pretty sure I won't care today." She said as she laughed like a little girl.

She was dressed in an all white pants suit, that fit her like a glove. The royal blue blazer and royal blue six inch heels set the outfit back fifty years her prime. The golden accessories that adorned her ears, neck and fingers were the things that kept everyone wondering,"how old is this woman?" .

Every time she stepped out of the house she was flawless and ageless.

"Now if this worked out like I know it will, this stadium should have at least one hundred thousand people in attendance. Not to mention all those who didn't get an invite to come inside."

"I Don't want to leave with regrets, so I apologize to you now if I have hurt your little feelings, but you didn't make the big picture of my journey Sweet Liver. You were loved and everything was done in preparation for today. So sit back and stop pouting, live your own life and you can take me out if you want. Just kidding, y'all of Sister Faith loves each of you the same. God has to use some of us as visual aide".

"Wouldn't it be funny if after going through all this preparation, I am speaking to three people today. The sound guy, the maintenance dude and the lady who bought a scouted ticket to enter."

She laughed so much, I think she snorted once or twice. It was so like Sister Faith to be telling jokes at her own funeral.

"I was sure of the plan for my life, I was a part of the preparation and planning process. If I did anything right you should be seeing it all come together right about now!"

"I know half of y'all sitting here like deer in headlights. And the other half are trying to look dignified like you understood perfectly what I just said and just like that you got it. Wake up people!".

"Listen, this presentation was not Sister Faith sitting in front of her phone recording herself at her desk. This was a production, lights make-up effects the whole nine. She was speaking from the very stage we are using today. It kinda freaked me out at first, but I was drawn into the environment that it didn't even matter. As the presentation continued she became more serious and we listened like our lives were hanging in the balance of a life already lived, now what does that say for us?"

"I know the question everyone is still wonder. How old is this woman? I promised myself after I turned eighty that every year belonged to God and I stopped counting. I stopped counting so long ago I forgot when it was. So I could be eighty-one or one hundred-eighty. Does it really matter?"

"I do want to take this time to tell you all who Sister Faith was, were I come from and how did I end up here. When I finally run out of words, I promise to take my seat to see if this life really ever ends".

<u>My Story</u>

"I was born Faith F. Christian the last of· five brothers and four sisters to Mr. Dieu Aide Christian and Mrs. Serviteur Aide Christian. My family was everything to me. I don't recall a bad, or negative event happening in or around my house until that day."

"Momma use to say God protected his special people to never endure worldly pain. She also said that the pain a servant endures comes with a hurt that is unexplainable, but it is endurable if you stay in the light."

"I was about five when that day came. Momma was cooking and singing as she always did after church on Sunday evenings. The boys were in the yard with Paw while the girls and I were playing dress up in Momma's closet."

"That day, I heard chaos for the first time in my life. I can still remember the fear that gripped my little heart when I heard the loud men yelling, the dogs barking uncontrollably and the gun shots ringing so near the window in Momma's bedroom."

"I heard the man tell Paw," "put your shot gun

down before I kill you old man." "Then I heard Paw say," "Mista, this here is my land, I own it free and clear. Everything that your eyes can see right now belongs to Mr. Dieu Christian. This here is my family and I will not bow to the likes of hate-filled sinners, in the mist of all my God has blessed me with. If it is my turn to die by your hand today Mista, believe this: The God I serve has already planned this out, he will win in the end no matter what".

"A very small boy sized man yelled out," "shoot the bastard!" "At this time a big man had come into the house and brought me and my sisters outside in to the yard." "I heard Momma screaming from inside the house, but they never let her come outside with the rest of us."

"When Paw heard Momma cry out his name he turned to all of us kids and said," "Today God's plan for one of you is being birthed. This will be the worst pain you will ever endure. Nothing else that the devil can send your way will prosper. The one who makes it through this will be the one to prove to the world God is real. I love each and every one of you, never forget that."

"As all of us stood there with tears in our eyes, Paw turned and said to the men," "leave my family be!'" and started shooting at them. "All I know is bodies started to drop to the ground. As Paw made his way to the front door of the house, I heard him say," "We go together Honey Chops!" "That's what he use to call Momma when they were playing around the house."

"After a small while had passed it was quiet. I didn't hear no voices, guns or dogs barking. I looked around to realize I was standing in the middle of my siblings bodies, as they laid lifeless in the yard.

Outside of that circle was the body of every man and dog that came to do us harm that day. On the porch of my family's home, Paw's lifeless arms held Momma's lifeless body. I was the only one left standing."

"I must have stood there for three night falls before I heard Momma's voice saying," "remember to look for the light when you get lost, remember to look for the light when you get scared and Baby-Dumpling, remember the light is the only way to always be with family in the end. So when you finally see the light keep your eyes on it."

"This is the first time I have ever spoken about that day to anyone. My husband and children have lived and died and never knew anything about that part of my history."

"As she wiped a few tears from her eyes she began to speak again."

Hear The Light

"A hunger like I have never felt before hit the pit of my stomach like boulders thrown off the cliff."

"I thought to myself maybe I can look to the light for food. As I looked around I couldn't find no light, so I stood there another night fall. Then it happened. I saw the light, it was so bright and beautiful. I knew at that moment I would be okay. I followed that light for hours. Waiting to hear it speak to me."

"Momma always told me that when I find the light to listen very carefully to the words it speaks to me. She told me to always obey the voice of the light. My Momma was the smartest most honest woman I have ever known, if she said the light will speak to me then I will wait until it does. I kept walking."

"I must have walked for four more night falls before I heard the light".

"Come to me child before you catch your death today." "As I focused my big brown eyes on the light an image of a little old lady appeared before me. She was dressed in an old house robe like Momma use to wear. I thought this has got to be the voice of the light, so I came to her."

"By the time I reached her personal space all I could remember was falling asleep."

"When I woke, it smelled like Momma was cooking Sunday breakfast again and everything I thought had happened was just a stupid nightmare."

"When I looked around the room I could see this was a strange place and I had no idea where I was."

"I began to cry uncontrollably and to my surprise the voice spoke and said,"

"Child hush all that crying there is nothing to harm you here."

"Instantly the fear was gone. Momma was right about the words spoken from the light. I felt so much better."

"The Voice of the light introduced herself to me by saying,"

"Hello Dumpling, I am Ms. Esperer and you can call me Momma E. What may I call you?"

"I stood up beside the bed and said you can call me Faith F. Christain thank you". "You should have heard the laughter that came from Momma E."

"Dumpling, I don't know how you got all the way out here. I am at least twenty miles from any kind of civilization. The Lord must be working, we are gonna live until we find out what he is up too".

"Momma E had a son, she called his name Amour. I loved the way it sounded every time she spoke it. Even as a child I always thought, the light had a way with words".

"She raised me and Amour as brother and sister. We would go to church together and when they started teaching folks how to read at the church house Amour and I would be the first ones in class. Then we would come home and show Momma E what we were taught that day. We would read her the Bible and she would say".

"Look at my babies, learning. You two are gonna make God proud one day. You will change the world"."Then she laughed a hardy laugh like my Momma use to when she thought she was telling us kids some secret that only her and the Lord knew about".

"When the light spoke those words, a feeling that I still haven't found words for came over my little frail body". "I began to remember Momma saying,"

"The light will bring a feeling like no other to your whole body. Don't be afraid. The light is filling you with everything you need to make it in life".

Feel The Light

"The next few years when we were at the church house I would see people jumping around and shouting. They would sing songs of praise to the Lord for all the good things he was doing".

"I thought to myself," "they must be feeling their lights right now, but mines was not working yet.

"I was a grown girl when Momma E went to spend time with my family. I knew she was going because she was the voice of the light".

"Amour and I were standing in that church house holding hands in front of a wooded bed for Momma E".

"I had no idea how I was gonna live without the voice of the light to guide me. I know I felt something once, but I didn't understand how I would feel it again if Momma E was no longer around".

"The preacher began to say so many good things about Momma E all the folks were crying with snot running from their noses. It was a site to see. Amour and I just watched and listened as the preacher spoke about love and never being alone. He turned to us and said".

"Momma E was a mother to us all. She requested that at the end of this ceremony that I would wed the two of you as husband and wife."

"I remember thinking he is trying to get us to laugh away our sorrows, because I ain't nobodies wife."

"Amour placed his large hand on my shoulder and looked down at me, he was well over six feet tall and I was only five feet myself".

"He said Momma would never lead us wrong, will you marry me?"

"Honey Muffins, Sister Faith felt something! It built up from my smallest toe and shocked every bit of hair on my body. It was at that moment I knew that I was feeling the light again. I started shouting and singing praise for all the good things the Lord was doing like all the other members did on Sunday mornings".

"If he can cause me to feel the light again, he must be the replacement voice for Momma E, so I will follow him to me my family again".

"Amour was a man of the Lord. After the first baby came, he began to preach at the church house on Friday night to all the young husbands. That quickly turned into a fish fry every weekend for the families of the husbands he would speak to over at the church house".

"By the time the twins came, I had seven children to tend to, a husband to protect and six families to cook for on the weekend".

"People use to ask me all the time how I was able to wear so many hats?" "All I could say was I follow the light and it all works out".

"Sweetness, when we reached baby number seventeen, Amour was the senior pastor at the church house and those six families became every family in our perish".

"When the woman would ask me now," "how do you do everything you do and still look amazing".

"I would respond by saying, The light is all I need to get everything accomplished each day."

"By the time Amour retired from the church

house we had been married twenty years. When he died I was lost without the voice or the feeling of the light again".

"At his funeral the preacher preached a message that said: The Lord is the Light of the world."

"Now I was confused, I have seventeen children and no husband and now after all these years you tell me that the Lord is the light".

"This day after he spoke he gave an alter call. He said". "Sometimes Momma and Daddy are the voice you need to follow, until you can hear the Lord your God for yourself, when his Holy Spirit connects with your spirit, you will begin to hear and feel things from on high. Say yes, to everything that comes from the Holy Spirit, follow him and you will see Pastor Amour again. Now if there is anyone here that has never met the Lord for yourself please, step forward".

"I know I have witnessed so many people going up to meet the Lord, but I never thought to try him for myself. I thought I had my light and my life was good, because Momma E and Amour spoke well for my light and everything was just what my Momma said it would be if I listened. I was just waiting for the day to see everyone again".

"As I found myself standing in front of the preacher, my hands began to sweat and my mouth got real dry. He asked me if I believed Jesus rose from the dead and took my sins so I can have a personal life with the Lord?"

"I answered yes sir I do".

"Then he said today you are a child of God, today you only hear his voice and follow his every command."

"Sweet Bug Nuggets, Sister Faith felt something, this time it was like nothing I had ever experienced before. The memories of all the people I loved and lost came flooding to my mind at that moment, I felt hurt, pain and anger that I had no clue was inside of me. I yelled out with everything in me. Lord save me!"

"Just like that I felt like a new woman, I began to teach the other widows on Friday nights down at the church house, then we would have a fish fry every weekend for the families of these widows".

"I did that for at least twenty years while raising seventeen children and I never had another husband".

"My children went on to be successful, Amour and I ended up raising Four doctors, Three nurses, three teachers, five preachers, three musicians, one writer and one law-man. I'd say we did good if you ask me".

"Looking back over the years if it wasn't for the light leading and guiding me I would have been lost".

"Speaking to you today I have out lived every single soul in my family line. I have buried all seventeen of my children in the span of five years and every grand-child that was birthed died before their second birthdays".

"At the ripe old age of eighty, I asked the Lord what now?"

"I promise like you are sitting in these seats captivated by every word I have said so far, the Lord responded," **"It's about time, I thought you would never ask!"**

"Sugar Lumps, as sure as I heard it, I laughed and I understood why my Momma and Momma E would laugh in the manor they did".

"It is from that moment that the Lord told me to prove his word without distraction or hinderance." "I thought to myself, what a mighty task for a little old lady, and the Lord replied,"

"You were born for this."

<u>Sister Faith's Ministry</u>

"After spending twelve months alone on my families farm, the Lord said it was time to leave, he told me to sell everything and move to the big city."

"I thought Lord you must be joking, I have never stepped foot in the big city a day in my life. I don't know how to function around no city folks."

"Let me tell you something Baby-Lamb, when the Lord speaks and you don't listen it is a very uncomfortable feeling in life."

"I was waiting to finish the sale of the farm but I was also dragging my feet for time. I held onto those papers for a month, until the chicken coupe caught a fire and darn near burned the whole farm to the bare ground".

"I got the message real quick. It was time for me to leave and move on to the big city."

"The nice lady who helped me sell my farm had also found me a nice small house in the big city near her daughter who was the wife of one of the wealthiest pastors in town."

"I was so pleased with my modest home, I

decorated it with things that reminded me of all of my loved ones who were waiting for me to finish my task so I can be with them again."

"Immediately I began to work in the church, I would sing, cook and clean. If I did all of these things to the glory of the Lord he would be pleased and I will be able to see my family again."

"Years went by and all I did was sing, cook and clean for thousands of people every week, I began to get tired for the first time in my life."

"One day I asked the Lord in prayer, please tell me what you want from me, I promise to give it to you in exchange to see my family again."

"With a hardy Momma laugh the Lord said,""**daughter you still don't get it.**"

"**When you were a girl tragedy hit your life and you went in search of the light your Momma told you about. Out of desperation when you saw the sun in the sky you began to follow it like your life depended on reaching its very location.**"

"**When you heard Momma E's voice you clung to her every word thinking it was the light** speaking to you. You followed her instructions to the letter."

"When Momma E left, you began to follow your husbands voice like it was your only hope."

"I thought you finally got the message when you gave your life to me at Amour's funeral. For the life of you, I still don't know what happened to us after that."

"Can you look back over the long life you lived without personally including me? Can you see how I kept you going fast and fierce for all those years."

"Faith, you are the perfect servant, you listen and follow instructions well."

"Now we finally make it to the best part and you are getting tired! My daughter this will work when you find out why you must follow my voice."

"With that said the Lord stopped speaking to me and I was left to find out my why?"

"Come to find out Sugar-Cubes, you all are my

why. At least you are a part of it."

"It took me more than three more years to figure out, that I was living to see my family again. There was nothing wrong with that in itself, but after reading the word and hearing the Lord speak through the word I realized He has been so good to my ignorant butt that I owe him everything."

"It wasn't my family that I longed to see. It was the God who had saved my family I was longing for."

"Eureka! I think she's got it! Now use everything to help me save a dying nation. Daughter you have the light and no one can stop you, do as I say and we will be together in no time."

"That evening there was a terrible storm out doors, everything in the big city had closed early. I sat on my screened in porch and had a grand conversation with the Lord. He began to explain every ministry represented here today. He shared all y'all business with me before I even met you. Precious Puppets, you were set up by the best!"

With a big old lady laugh that sent chills through my body, she continued with her story while over one hundred thousand people listened with attentive ears.

"I had know idea how I was gonna pull off so much work with my little old self." "Then it hit me! Like a bolt of lighting that was filling the dark skies above. It was as if the Lord opened my mouth and poured his words in."

"Needless to say my own words were coming out my back end. The back-end in the spirit of course. Meaning, my words were nothing but…"

The crowd all gasped at the same time, it was crazy to witness the people and their responses to a dead woman.

"Mess… nothing but mess! Like I told several of you time and time again; stop serving your mess to the Lord's babies."

"I use to ask the Lord to create a spiritual enema, to get all this mess out his body."

"The problem is, we don't eat right. Yes, yes we get the word, but y'all done added all this extra stuff to it."

"All these preachers have turned into mad

scientists mixing up concoctions for the body, then you wonder why we so sick."

"They putting additives and preservatives in the food and look what happened with that; cancer, diabetes, AIDS." "Our bodies were not made to process this man made junk."

"Additives and preservatives are added to foods so that they can keep and stay fresh longer." "The Lord's word is always fresh it don't need nothing added to it."

"Your right, you are absolutely right... It's not my time to preach... I bet those of you who made the joke that I would preach my own funeral are not laughing now are ya!" "You know I can do it babies... but I won't."

<u>Why Faith?</u>

Music started playing and another slide show of pictures began to flood the screens. You could hear the voices in the crowd when they saw themselves show up as part of the slide show presentation.

When Sister Faith reappeared on the screen, she was dressed in an all white dress that fit her beautifully. Her makeup was flawless and her hair was down. It was the first time I had ever seen her hair down. She always wore sassy wigs or a plain bun. I never knew she had at least twenty-four inches of beautiful shiny pure silver hair. She looked like an angel standing there on the screen.

As if she could hear the comments of the crowd, she waited until they faded, then she began to speak again.

"Well, Love Muffins, This is the last of Sister Faith as you know her. My journey ends here today." "My destiny has been fulfilled and now it is time to fulfill yours".

"If you did the math like I tried to, you would know I am well over one hundred and twenty years old. How much older, is the first question I will ask the Lord to answer when I get to heaven."

"Look around again, see all the faces in the crowd, these are the Lord's people. Help each other remain focused on the voice of the Lord, teach each other what he has personally spoken to you. Encourage each other when life gets your fellow saints down and out."

"Talk to the Lord so y'all can figure out your why. Here is a secret… the how and how long is left totally up to you."

"Lord, I have done all that you have required of me, I have wasted precious years and could have reached so many more of your lost people. Lord, I repent of my ignorance. Lord, please take these people which you have given for me to serve and create in each of them your ministry. In your name I pray, amen."

After her prayer the screen when black, and fireworks started to fill the skies above the stadium. Trumpets and drums started playing and it was sonorous.

The screens then displayed: Intermission.

__Intermission__

No one in attendance moved or spoke a word for at least five minutes. It was like everyone at the same time had a moment of silence that was not on the program.

Over the loud speaker a deep voice rang out saying, "You may fellowship for the next fifteen minutes". Instantly the crowd began to mingle and talk to one another.

The next thing on my instructions was to find five people with a purple rose. Now, there were over one hundred thousand people here, how was I gonna find five purple roses? As I started walking around the stadium, people began to stop me to say what a wonderful job I was doing as officiator of the service. They tried to tell me their Sister Faith stories, but I was on a mission. I had to find five needles in this great big haystack.

One young lady stopped me in my tracks and said, "Hello, I think I am supposed to see you at this time for further instructions."

When I looked up she had a purple rose on the lapel of her jacket. This wasn't going to be hard at all, they are looking for me too. I explained to her I had to find four more people and then I could open my next letter. She laughed and said,"it's just like Sister Faith to send everyone on a wild goose chase".

We both laughed and I requested that she come to the center of the field with me in hopes to draw the other rose carriers my way. As we moved closer to the field, four others came right behind us.

When they reached me and this woman they all explained their instructions stopped with, find the officiator during intermission. After introductions, I opened my final note from Sister Faith and it read:

To My Sugar Plums:

This is it, Eulogy time! Now don't start that worrying in your little heads.

Your assignment was to show up, congratulations! That part was a success. See you can be obedient when you want to. Lol

In this moment we need you to be honest with the people in attendance today. Dedicate every second that you have lived on this earth to the Lord. Leave the podium empty, my Lord will re-fill you.

1. Stacy - pray for the circle of grace
2. Reverend Allen Turnbell - Luxure
3. Bishop Helen Cooper - Avidite
4. Apostle Bishop Overseer Thomas Goode Phd - Fierte
5. Pastor Sheldon Gram - Insecurite
6. Evangelist Helen Stackhouse - Selfmoord

Stacy your assignment is to preach my eulogy. You can do this!

Each of you should know how special you are to me and the Lord. We need you today, let go and let God. No cliche intended. This is the real deal babies!

Forever Love

Sister Faith F. Christian

After I read the letter aloud, each person took a moment to look over it for themselves. No one had a clue what the words she had written beside each name meant. While we stood there waiting for the longest fifteen minutes to pass, the ministers began to pull out bible apps and began scribbling on their programs.

The people were all over the place, sharing stories about how they met Sister Faith and how she changed their lives and ministries. Come to find out every person in attendance was a preacher of the gospel.

One lady had a tattered piece of paper that she held onto for forty years. After she showed it to a few people everyone realized they had signed that very same agreement.

Sister Faith's Ministry Agreement

I, <u>Sister F. Christian</u> agree to deliver the word of the Lord to: <u>Name of Church</u>

You, <u>Preacher's Name</u>, agree to keep an open mind and heart to receive the message in what ever format it is given.

I, <u>Sister Faith F. Christian</u> will stay with your ministry for three days.

You, <u>Preacher's Name</u> agree to pray and fast everyday I am involved with your ministry.

You, <u>Preacher's Name</u> will donate <u>$ set dollar amount</u> to the Sister Faith Project.

You must also agree that on the day I am sent off from this earth, you, <u>Preacher's Name</u> will attend my service. Please explain to your congregation that if you pass before me the most senior minister is to attend to represent your ministry.

Sealed in the Blood

X _Sister Faith F. Christian_
X <u>Preachers Name</u>

THE EULOGY

A five minute time clock showed up on the big screens. I can't speak for anyone else but, my stomach was doing flips and cartwheels and some more stuff. It was three minutes left when Bishop Cooper said, "Let's pray and maybe we will hear the voice from the light". Everyone laughed, but you could feel the tension that was building in each of us.

I guess it was time for me to start my part and pray:

Lord, we know who you are for ourselves thanks to your servant, Sister Faith. Please pour your words in our mouths like a spiritual enema. Let everything that is not about you leave the spiritual back end. Use us Lord, to continue your work as Sister Faith finally gets the rest she deserves. We are your vessels, to be used at your discretion. Lord, we humble ourselves and exult you at this time. We submit our voices to only your message today, in the name of our Lord, amen.

Five, four, three, two….
Help us Lord!

Luxure

Reverend Allen walked to the podium, he looked to be about fifty-five. He was a tall drink of water, dark beautiful skin, silky jet black hair and brown eyes like you have never seen. He was dressed in a burgundy two piece suit that was custom fit. If I wasn't trying to live right?...

I'm sorry I don't know where that came from. I am on a mission for the Lord right now, pull it together Stacy!

He grabbed the mic and began singing. "We love you Lord, We need you Lord". About the third time, the entire stadium was singing those words. I could feel the atmosphere change. The more we sung the heavier the air would get. I thought I was gonna faint. Around the tenth time the verse was sung, I felt like I was floating in the air.

Now I know I stopped smoking funny sticks when I met Sister Faith, it can't possibly still be in my system.

As he brought the song to a close, I felt like a different person, I can't tell you exactly what that means but I liked it. It was comfortable and relaxing and in some ways I just felt free and clean.

"Good evening, I am Reverend Allen Turnbell of God's House Ministries located in St. Louis. I too signed one of those Sister Faith Agreements about ten years ago".

"I have to remember the famous word's of Sister Faith,"don't preach Al when they tell you to bless the food." So I will honor her by just telling you how Sister Faith touched my life and ministry".

"I had a pastor friend from Africa, he told me a woman came to his church for three days, two days she just looked around and asked many questions.

He was beginning to worry if he had done the right thing by allowing her access to his ministry in this way. On the last day he said she spoke a message, that dealt with every issue that had been hindering his ministry. He said he listened to the old lady and did what she said. He told me the following Sunday, his congregation had tripled in size and replenishes itself yearly."

"I had to have this old lady come and triple my ministry".

"Yes, I said it. Tripling my ministry was what I wanted from her. See I had a problem with wanting too much of a good thing. Don't get me wrong my motivation for ministry started out to please the Lord. Then he blessed me with so much I started loosing sight of why I was doing what I was doing".

"The people gave me a huge home, more money than I had ever seen, cars I still can't pronounce and women. I had my pick of the finest church goers who always found their way to the front row of every service".

"My church was good, my preaching was flowing, but I had an ache in my heart that I could not shake."

"After a long crying out for help prayer, I called Sister Faith. I asked if she would be in the St. Louis area anytime in the near future and I would love to have her come visit".

"She explained that her time was priceless, but she could be in St. Louis in three days. She told me to fast and pray from the time we hang up the phone until she was standing in front of me. She also told me that I would have to give her $50,000 when she arrived".

"I thought she must be loosing her mind if she thinks I will pay her $50K of my hard earned money so she can preach in my house. She didn't even have a church of her own and I have never heard of her".

"After an awkward silence, she said call your church leaders together for a three day shut-in. Do not explain or answer any questions. On the third day, schedule your entire congregation to attend a special service just for them. Again do not explain or answer any questions. When we hang up this phone you will begin to fast and pray".

"Before I could say a word, she hung up the phone. Now I thought this must be a joke my African friend is playing on me. She did not know where we are located in St. Louis, she did not know what ministry I was calling from, and she is seriously crazy if she thinks I will pay her $50K for dropping orders on me, for my house."

"I was all set to move on with the rest of my life and see how I was gonna fit this bazaar story in my next sermon. I hope you can hear the real of what I was thinking at the time". "I know we all preachers but this is were I was at the time".

"About three minutes after that call a messenger came into my office with a package addressed to me. I signed for the item and closed the door behind him so I could open it in private".

"Some of the nice ladies in church would send me goodies from time to time and everyone didn't need to see my blessing, after all I was the man of the Lord".

"When I opened the package it contained a plaque that read: To Reverend Allen Turnbell for your faithfulness in ministry. There was a note and a check for $50K. The note was from the Children's Nation Ministry in Africa. It said thank you for all your support in building our city when we had nothing. Today we have all we need and more. Take this money and use it for yourself, not ministry it is for you, your friends in Africa".

"Instantly Sister Faith's voice rang in my ear … begin to fast and pray. I don't know if I was inspired by the Lord or scared out of my mind, but I started to fast and pray. I called the leaders like she told me to and gave the order to set the service".

"I thought if this lady is real, I will be blessed, but if she is a no show, I will go to the islands with a few congregation sisters to assist me while I take a sabbatical".

"For the next three days I stayed locked up in

my office fasting and praying. If I can be transparent with you, it was hard for the first day. I wanted so bad to talk on the phone or look at social media. Several times I wanted to leave the office to get food.

The next morning when I woke up, I thought wow! I made it overnight. This day was easier, I began to read my bible and that turned into looking into study books. By the third day I was on fire. I wanted to preach to somebody about my experience.

"I showered and dressed to meet Sister Faith. At this time I was hoping she was real, but she still never got my contact information".

"Monday, twelve noon a little old lady walked in my office and said," "Al, we have got a lot of work to do around here".

"All I could say was, Yes Ma'am! She had eyes that looked straight through you, it felt like I could not hide anything from her if I tried".

"I started to tell her about my experience over the last three days and she didn't seem to be one bit interested in what I had to say".

"What time will the leaders arrive and how many will be joining us?" "Is what she asked as she rudely interrupted my story."

"I told her I have thirty-two leaders and they will be here by two, but I don't know how many will show with such short notice and no explanation".

"She replied only the Lord's true leaders are designed to show up, that's why you had to fast and pray the spectators away. The Lord wants to prove himself to you Al. You have destiny and it can start right now or you can waste your best years on yourself".

"I was feeling exposed by this lady. It was very uncomfortable to say the least. Sitting in the Lord's oven is no walk in the park. I asked what will we do when the leaders arrive, should I prepare something real quick?"

"She laughed and said if you could have prepared something I would not be here! We need you to sit down and only speak when spoken to. You have said enough foolishness for one lifetime".

"Yes, ma'am, is all I could say".

"At 2:15 Sister faith said," "lock the church up,

no one enters or leaves until it is time". Evangelist Neil yelled out, "What time is that!"

"Sister Faith looked at him and we all heard it. Her lips didn't move nor did she flinch or bat an eye,"

"You better sit down and shut up!" With that look he locked the doors and we all took seats in the sanctuary.

I watched as 13 leaders found spots to themselves around the large sanctuary. Sister Faith was walking around talking to each person individually. No one knew what she said to the person before them. It took her until the next morning to reach all the leaders.

"It was noon the second day and Sister Faith finally got around to ministering to me, I was ready to hear, what thus saith the Lord."

"Al, where is my check"? "Is what this woman had the nerve to say to me after she has ministered all night to my leadership. Here I was on day five with no food and she is worried about money".

"I took the check I had gotten in the package and signed it over to Faith Christian. I reluctantly gave her the check, and she knew it."

Sister Faith, smiled and placed the check in her purse and said, "Al, you have sown in the flesh, now may the Lord bless you in the spirit. We need all of you to pray for your followers, your congregation in its entirety until further notice".

"She laughed and said, if you are never told to stop praying for them, then you never stop praying for them".

"Let me wrap this up and take my seat. On the third day at 12 noon, Sister Faith said to have the doors of the church opened."

"I did as I was told and the congregation started to pour in and fill the empty seats. She asked, "How many official members do you have?" I proudly said 1300 active members."

"It was 12:15 and Sister Faith said lock the doors, the Lord is about to minister to this house specifically."

"There was no singing, no prayer, no nothing. She stood behind my sacred desk and said,""please, stand if this is your first time with this ministry.

One young lady that looked to be about twenty-five, stood up. She was drop dead gorgeous, A perfect feminine body, long hair and a beautiful angelic face. She was the perfect blessing from the Lord for me.

I'm keeping everything real with you today. I had been crying out to the Lord, fasting, praying and in one vision, my mind went straight back to the reason we are all here today.

Sister Faith asked her," "do you know anyone here today? The young girl said no, ma'am, I don't. Sister Faith then said, look around do you know anyone here? The girl responded no Ma'am."

"Sister Faith told her to come to where she was standing. I knew she was not going to let this little girl stand behind my sacred desk. I don't even know her.

If you know Sister Faith, that is exactly what she did. The girl went to the podium and Sister Faith said tell this ministry what brought you here."

"The girl began to weep as she spoke".

"I am really not sure why I came here today, I was walking in the park when I saw people coming into the church. I thought I might as well go too, maybe I will find the answers to living a better life."

"When I was younger my mom was a preacher, she would spend all of her time praying and working in the church. My dad was the head deacon.

I watched people pull them in so many directions. I knew the Lord wasn't playing a part in this circus. The more money they took in the more they spent. They would buy stuff and call it blessings.

My dad, the deacon would take women on prayer retreats all the time, while mom would sit back like she didn't see what was going on around her.

I thought to myself when I can get away from my parents and this church stuff, I will be better off.

I remember the last sermon I heard my mom preach in that church. It was called: The Lust you Love, she preached like I had never heard in my life. All the people in the church were shouting so loud I could barely hear her end the message.

She ended with this: The lust you love is keeping

you from a Lord to serve. You can have what ever you want, the choice is totally up to you, but this day you must decide, the lust you love or a Lord to serve.

"People in the congregation began to weep and cry out, I am sorry Lord!"

"At the sound of this girls voice, I fell to my knees and begged the Lord for forgiveness. For the next hour the entire place erupted with prayers of repentance from every corner of the building.

"Five hours later, I felt an urgency to close the service, if that's what this was. I looked around and Sister Faith was no where to be found. The Lord has spoken to his people, amen! As the congregation began to leave, I requested the leaders stay behind to reflect."

"In my office stood thirty-two leaders. Elder Smith asked, where were all of you three days ago? I stopped him and said, If you did not come when I requested, from this moment until otherwise noted you are released from your church leadership duties. You don't have to leave the church, only exclude yourself from further leadership duties. You all may go home now, we will discuss everything in detail next week."

"I was left with 13 leaders standing in amazement in my office. I told them how I encountered Sister Faith and what led up to that very moment. Each leader after me began to share the experience she had with each of them.

Every leader including myself had been struggling with some type of lust. For some it was money, others things, but most of us had a sexual lust that was mind controlling. After confessing to one another our transgressions we held hands to pray, promising each other we would never allow that spirit to function in our mist again.

Here I am ten years later with 300 leaders and 13K members. That week my life changed, every bit of fear I had about being exposed was gone, I came clean in that office to 13 true men and women of the Lord. To this day we cover each other and we have never stopped praying for the Lord's ministry."

That young lady who ministered that day is now my wife of seven years. The Lord has a way of blessing us better than the blessings we create ourselves and reward ourselves with.

"I promise you, every time any type of lustful thought tries to invade my mind, Sister Faith and my wife's voices sing in harmony, The Lust You Love… and I promise you as I stand her today, instantly those thoughts are changed to praise for what the Lord has delivered me from and for the blessings he has created for me.

Those thoughts no longer have me bound! I asked the Lord, if I am delivered why keep temptation around. He replied, **it's all in your perception. It can be labeled temptation or it can be labeled as a praise opportunity. The choice is yours to make.**

As I take my seat, my life today, is a testament for the work of Sister Faith. I don't even think I will miss her, because she is a forever part of our ministry the Lord entrusted us with and she is forever a part of my life.

<u>Avidite</u>

Praise the Lord saints. I am Bishop Helen Cooper and I promise not to be before you long. If Sister Faith was a stickler for anything, it was a preacher doing too much with the microphone. So I will share a brief Sister Faith encounter with you today.

I met Sister Faith twenty years ago. I was a struggling pastor of a very small congregation when she joined our three day revival. I remember the first question she asked me during lunch of the first day. What are we being revived from and what are we being released to?

I had no idea what she was asking so I just told her to pay close attention during the services and if she didn't get an answer on her own to come back to see me.

She said, "Okay Sugar Bear, I will."

I thought she was strange the way she moved around and spoke to people. I asked the head deacon if he knew who she was or where she came from? No one had ever seen this lady before.

The third day to end the services I asked if

anyone had any prayer requests. Why in the world did I do that. Sister Faith said yes I do and walked right up to the podium and started praying. The deacons asked if they should stop her, but I thought no, I will use this as a teaching tool later.

She began to pray that the Lord remove greed from the house and restore the spirit of giving. Her prayer was quick and to the point. Then she said now people of the Lord give.

I promise you that night we collected $10K. I could not believe we collected all that money. On a good day we may collect $1K half of which is tithes from a hand full of faithful members.

She asked if she could have a word with me in private. I took her to my office to talk. She told be that I was the reason the ministry is not giving properly.

She told me straight like this: Honey Toes, you are greedy and the Lord don't like that. You want more than you need and you take more than your share and you don't give with a good heart.

I was shocked that this lady had the nerve to come in my office and speak to me in that manner. She laughed that Sister faith Laugh and said, "Yes I am talking to you."

Thats your problem now people won't tell you the truth. Because you are the pastor you test your theory's first. If you think the Lord is saying give, you give first and if you need people to give more, you give more first. You greedy and you need to change.

I was instantly convicted, because I was greedy. I would say let's give to this and that and I would never put in. I even stopped paying tithes because I thought it's all the Lord's money anyway why do the extra step by putting it in the basket for it to be given to me anyway.

I confessed to her that day in my office. As I poured my heart out to this woman, she stopped me mid-sentence and said, If you believe you can change give me all the money you took in the last three services.

You have got to be kidding me, is what I yelled out loud. You want me to give you over $10K and I don't know you from Adam or Eve? She looked me straight in my eyes and said yes I do!

I thanked her for joining us over the last three days and informed her I was not going to be able to give her the money. I felt like I was in a spiritual robbing.

She left that night and for the next twelve months we collected under $200 per month. We at least use to collect $500 in tithes every month and now that was down to $125 in tithes and the rest was from offerings.

At this time my husband and I were supporting the ministries bills, which led to our personal expenses getting so behind. We owed the bank, our family and friends. It became embarrassing to say the least. We could not figure out for the life of us what was happening and why.

The next year at our annual three day revival we had a three guest speakers from France. The first day the minister preached: Ten Thousand Blessing for the Giver. The second minister preached: More of the Lord gets all of His Stuff. The final minister preached, "How Much is Too Much". Just like in the Bible when the rooster crowed three times and Peter was finally convicted, well so was I.

I could not wait to get home to send Sister Faith a check for $10K. It wiped out my savings and 401k, but I didn't care I realized at that moment in the service I didn't need anything as much as I need the Lord and if giving this money away shows my commitment to change then I will be a broke servant of the Lord.

Now you know that didn't make since you can never be broke and serve the Lord He is a repairer and healer. The Lord makes everything whole and right.

Once Sister Faith received the check she called me and said. "Rock-Head, we are proud of you. You know the level of greed you were operating from and you decided to change, may the blessings of the Lord fall without hinderance in your life," with those words she hung up the phone.

Let me tell you today I want for nothing, we collect over $10K every month in tithes and even more in offerings. My husband and I began to pay our tithes and offering again and that's when the overflow started pouring in. Sometimes we get caught up in the rituals and the stuff we do, that we forget we are forever servants and examples of how to serve the Lord and others.

Sister Faith was the first believer who loved the Lord enough to tell me the truth and for that she will forever be a part of my life and ministry. Sister Faith this Rock-Head finally got it!

Fierte

Greeting in the year of our Lord, I am Apostle Bishop Overseer Thomas Goode Phd, and I had the great pleasure of socializing with Sister Faith Christian one year ago today.

He stopped speaking and started to cry as he looked out over all the ministers and preachers who where attentively waiting to hear his Sister Faith story. As he wiped his face and cleared his nose and throat he began to speak again.

Hello, I am Thomas. It is not until right at this moment I actually heard the message she delivered to me one year ago this very day. He began to cry out in repentance. You had to be there to feel the electricity that began to flow throughout the stadium.

The other ministers on the podium began to assist Bishop Thomas. As he gained his composure he walked to the microphone again. This time he began to sing these words:

No matter how big I get, I will never be anything in comparison to you Lord.

If I ever find myself comparing me to another, I will stop. I will praise you and humbly proceed.

That is a song my grandmother sang to me everyday of my life until I was eighteen years old. Today, right now I get it. Forty years from the last time she sang it to me and now I get it.

I didn't have the regular Sister Faith experience. We met on a flight to Germany last year. She asked me if she could sit next to the window. I paid $45 extra to have the larger window seat, she had some nerve asking for it.

I looked into those eyes and said, yes ma'am you may sit next to the window. After we both were adjusted and the flight began, she asked what I did for a living.

Why did she ask that, I told her my bio, resume, certification, degrees, diary and journal? When I was coming up being a big time minister was what you wanted. The bigger the building; the bigger your home; the bigger your car; and the best assortments of fine attire was how you measured a successful ministry.

Don't get me wrong we loved the Lord and started out sincerely in the Lord's service. Life has a way to set the most educated preacher up for a fall.

I promise you the Lord is ministering to me now in your mist.

I told Sister Faith about all the good work I did and all the dreams I had of being one of the greatest preachers of our time.

I am gonna take everyones word today that she was talkative and witty, because on a fifteen hour flight we had several conversations. I must have been talking the entire time because after her first question, she didn't speak again until we were about to land.

As I was standing to let her gather her things to leave, she said, do you like jokes? I said yes ma'am. She asked me: what's the difference between today's Pastors and King Nebuchadnezzar?

I was stumped, I asked what's the difference? She said, pastors don't literal stay with animals and they never shut up. She laughed that laugh and walked down the aisle.

Message notifications stated to hit my phone and I never thought about that joke until today.

If I rewind seven months before that flight I was on a preaching circuit along with twenty pastors from around the world. We had to audition to join this extraordinary team of preachers with vocabularies that are larger than life itself. I thought I would easily advance on the circuit, I was none other than: "Apostle Bishop Overseer Thomas Goode Phd".

It was my first year and every stop I had to preach in the mental institutions. The other pastors were preaching in stadiums and arenas. I had five and six people who were late taking their medication.

After going to the board and asking if there were another area for me to serve. To my surprise they did. They offered me hall duty. The person on hall duty watches and prays in silent all day every day.

Do you think Apostle Bishop Overseer Thomas Goode Phd, was gonna sit in silence. I think not, I preached to those mental patience like no bodies business. I didn't even have to study or prepare a sermon, they were drugged and couldn't hear me anyway. Or so I thought.

You are not going to believe this, but right before I reached the microphone the first time, I got a text message from one of the board members saying, We thank you for your service and we noticed how you humbly served the Lord's people no matter their social status. We would like you to lead our summer sessions.

What you saw was my most inner secret sins came to the light front and center. I din't take the job to preach because it was the godly thing to do. I took it because I was not gonna waist my time and talent sitting in silence. I was not thinking about the prayer part. I just wanted to be heard.

My grandma's song and Sister Faiths joke today changed my heart. I understand humility. You know the worst part about a fortified pride life? You are always a target, you never get to make a mistake, have a bad day or just feel bad. The fortified pride life is a trap. If you see it in fellow saints, let's not discuss it. Let's just humble ourselves and pray. As I leave you laughing at that joke and knowing the punch line, I will leave you with these words.

No matter how big you get, You will never be anything in comparison to the Lord.

If you ever find yourself comparing you to another, please yield. Start a praise and humbly proceed.

Insecurite

As Bishop Goode walked away from the microphone still singing his grandmother's song. Pastor Gram exchanged greetings and they changed positions on the stage.

Good day saints, I am Pastor Sheldon Gram of Jesus is Real Ministry. Sister Faith came to my church sixteen years ago this month. It was the last night of our Annual Revival Conference.

I was so glad it was the last day for services, I had a headache that would make a mannequin take two aspirin. Saints, the pounding in my head made it difficult to say anything or focus on anything for too long. I had one of my pastor friends from Texas close out the services for me. I am pretty sure it was an excellent message he had the congregation on their feet and totally engaged in the words he projected into their spirits.

I on the other hand was contemplating if I should go to the hospital to see about this different type of head pounding I was experiencing. As my pastor friend reached the end of his message, the place was so loud, I could not take it anymore. I dismissed myself and went into my office for water and aspirin.

One of the Deacons came to assist me, but I insisted I would be okay and that he should return to the services. As I sat in my office I prayed a quick prayer, Lord you are the healer of this body. I trust you with all that I am and ever hope to be. Please release me from this agony in my head. In your name I pray, amen.

I laid my head down on my desk in my dark office for some relief. I didn't hear anything for about five minutes, I was guessing the service was over. But how is everyone gone and the place is so quiet so fast? When I lifted my head to go investigate, this woman was standing in front of my desk and the lights were on.

Excuse me ma'am, is there something I can help you with? She said no sir, there is much I am about to help you with.

I didn't understand what was happening at this time my head was spinning in a cloud of confusion. I was thinking I could be dreaming. It felt peaceful so I let it happen.

Sister Faith introduced herself to me and explained that the Lord sent her into my church and into my office to deliver a message just for me. Until today, no one has ever known what happened in that office.

I never felt the need to share my experience because I was truly delivered and I saw no need to tell everyone what I had been dealing with. All I needed was for people in my congregation to know the struggles I dealt with internally. I was the pastor and I was supposed to have it all together. At lease that's what I was thinking until today, I feel the need to publicly share what the Lord has delivered me from, but I digress, let me get back to Ms. Faith.

You know us block-head preachers do that from time to time get off subject to prove that we know stuff as Ms. Faith would say.

After she introduced herself I felt like I had already met her. I asked if she had ever visited my church before and she responded, "Honey, if I had visited your church before you wouldn't be sitting in here with a heavy mind trying to figure out whats happening to your life.

Now Sheldon, you are the prime example of being too smart for your own good. Let me ask you one question, do you think the Lord would make you live an impossible life before people, but hide in open sight? I think not!

I asked, what do you mean hide in open sight? She continued, You are sitting here in this office questioning if you are the right man for the job. Contrary to popular beliefs, the Lord put you in this position and not man. Until you remember what got you to this point you will never be able to move towards your full potential and reach your ordained destiny.

It is perfectly fine to not have all the answers and to not be able to fix every issue. That has not been or never was your job. Your assignment is to lead the Lord's people to him while living an honest life of example. Sometimes examples mean trial and error learning. But for the life of me I will never understand how we become leaders and eureka! We are magical perfect specimens of every situation.

When you sleep at night and you toss and turn and question yourself and every decision you have made throughout the day, you are not demonstration the faith that got you here. Then you worry about what people think about you and your main goal is for everyone to celebrate you and honor your works you have a problem.

Do you remember as a child wanting to be the

line leader in school? Do you know what the job of the line leader was? The line leader was the kid who walked quietly and straight to the destination following all the teachers instructions. Everyone who followed the line-leader was supposed to follow suit. They were to walk quietly to the destination.

If the line-leader was out of order the entire line was out of order. Thus the reason why being the line leader was a great assignment to have, but the kid holding the position had great responsibilities to control the followers by example.

Now Mr. Pastor, you have been called to be the line-leader of your congregation. You follow the instructions of the Lord and lead the line to the destination. If someone gets out of order it is not your job to fix them the teacher will handle that you just keep walking and being the best example you can be.

Your head is all messed up because you keep looking at yourself and trying to figure out why the rest of the line is in disarray. All you need to know is that the teacher still has all authority and is still ultimately responsible for the entire line. When leaders forget that they are not the final authority we end up sitting in dark offices wondering what we did or are doing wrong. Most of the time the teacher picks the worst kid to be line-leader to prove to themselves that they can do something different from what they are use to. It's the same in your situation. The Lord knows your insecurities and he never meant for you to be perfect, just willing to try his way.

The pressures that you inflict on yourself is way out of the scope of your assignment. You are still a student who has to make it from one destination to another with minimal problems. If something happens along the way to the students at the end of the line, it is not your fault or your responsibility as long as you do what is right and continue to the destination.

I know this is elementary teachings and I don't mean to offend your status and knowledge, but sometimes leaders just need to know that you are your only responsibility, you were not equip to fix everything. The Lord has all that under control.

So, stop blaming yourself for what others are doing wrong, even the Lord allows people to work within their own wills and if he don't interfere, why would you.

Sometimes trying to fix stuff and people actually

hinders their process to becoming a line-leader themselves. Do your part and thats enough.

Do you understand what I am telling you Pastor?

Even though she spoke to me like I was a child I heard and understood the message. I had been beating myself up for years trying to figure out why my congregation was not growing in the Lord and why we always had ridiculous issues in and around the ministry.

I would question myself and blame myself for all the things that didn't look right in the ministry, I was responsible for these people. How could I be a successful line-leader and my people are not living for the Lord?

I studied more, prayed more, created classes and events that would help my people change. I eventually grew to be well known and loved in the religious community by my personal ministry was failing. It had to be my fault and the Lord had to be displeased with my actions.

Several times I though about giving up and just walking alone I thought at least that way I would only be responsible for me. That day was the day I decided to pass the ministry on to the assistant pastor and live out the rest of my days fulfilling personal ministry along the way.

She left me with these words that forever changed my life: A walk with the Lord is completely individual and absolutely a joint venture. When you understand that you will be able to do your part without the stress of trying to do everyones part.

She prayed with me and left a check for $10K on my desk. She told me to take that money and rebuild the line I was destine to lead.

I did exactly that, I took that money and put a down payment on a smaller building that we would own in five years. I began to be a servant of the Lord instead of trying to be the Lord in the flesh. I found out that me living a life pleasing to the Lord was all I had to do, all of my insecurities went away and I began to live a free life. As I put these practices into action my congregation began to do like wise, all of the bickering and fighting stopped, everyone began to love unconditionally and walk worthy of the Lord's calling.

Saints, we do have to walk alone each one of us, and at the same time we are all walking towards the same destination. I see you all today, but I hope to see you all at the Lord's designated destination. Pray for me as I pray for you. If Sister Faith could walk her lonely walk and still affect all of our lives we can do it too.

Selfmoord

Good Evening Saints, I am Evangelist Helen Stackhouse of Greater Life and Love International Ministries. I guess I should tell my Sister Faith story too.

I need to let you know what led up to me meeting Sister Faith. It was Monday morning and I was not feeling like myself. I had been feeling bad for a while but this morning was the worst. I called my doctor to see if I could drop in for a quick check up.

When I arrived in his office I had a temperature of 104 degrees. They tried franticly to bring my temperature down, but it was not budging. They transported me to the ER to be seen. I was admitted that morning and I was not released until Friday evening.

Now I had been in the hospital for five days and my husband Timothy came to see me the first day. He called the second day, and if you know his wear-a-bouts the other three days you would have been doing better than me.

I started to drive home as I thought to myself, what can I do now? I think I blacked out for a while, I had been crying buckets of tears. When I realized I was still in the car, I was parked outside of my church office.

I went into the empty sanctuary and laid on the floor. I cried out to the Lord, why? Why like this Lord? I have obeyed your word, I have labored and served your people. What will I do now? I am the leader of this ministry, how can I tell them this news. What will they think of me? Will I still be able to preach? How can I preach like this, when my life is over? So many thoughts, so many emotions ran through my mind.

I knew at that moment my life had to end that day. Little to my surprise it did, but not in the manner that I was thinking.

I laid on the floor for four hours crying and begging the Lord to remove this burden from my life. I reminded him of all the good I did and all the bad I avoided. I just could not understand for the life of me, Why do right if something like this can happen?

As I contemplated how I was going to quickly end this messed up life, my phone rang. I know this makes for an interesting story, but this was my real experience. The phone rang, it displayed unknown number, so I allowed it to go to voicemail.

I received the voicemail notification and I ignored it. As I focused my mind back to forming my final plan of ending my life. Text message notifications started coming through back to back.

I checked the messages and they read: PICK UP THE PHONE THE LORD HAS A BETTER PLAN! Not only was I freaked out by the texts coming from a number I had never seen before I forgot what I was about to do and felt the need to get to the person on the other end of these messages.

I sat there with my phone in my hand waiting for the unknown number to dial me back. Listen, I sat there with a blank mind waiting for the unknown to tell me what to do. Can you say desperate? I was ready to try what ever the unknown person wanted to suggest. It had to be better than my choice.

After an hour and thirteen minutes of sitting in complete silence with no thoughts running through my mind. I found myself in a rested state. It was like in that very moment, I couldn't form a thought if I wanted to. I didn't think about the diagnosis I was given, I didn't think about what I was going to do about the diagnosis. I didn't even think about the fact that I was about to kill myself.

In that last thought a fear gripped my soul to its core. With the quickness I had to repent. Lord, no matter what this world delivers to my door I will never again try to dishonor you by trying to alter this life in anyway. I have served you through some tough times and you have always seen me through. Lord, I trust you will fix it as you always do. Amen.

While I was exhaling the phone rang and nearly killed me. I thought Lord, you're gonna let me die of a heart attack instead, yeah that's better. I laughed to myself as I answered the phone.

You know how everyone has been speaking of that laugh that seems like you have a secret with the Lord. Believe me it is real. If you ever see a saint in a bad situation and they laugh a sly little laugh that you can't understand. Understand this, they are dealing with the Lord himself and they know it.

I said hello, how may I help you?

This loud little voice said, "Fast and pray until I get there". Lock yourself in the space you are in now and stay in place until I arrive, I will tell you what to do next when I get to you.

I asked, may I ask who I have the pleasure of speaking to? She replied, "I am Sister Faith and it's about to go down in a real way in your life. Fast and pray until I see you." Then she just hung up the phone in my ear.

Just as I was thinking, what in the world is this Lord? The phone rang again and nearly gave me my second heart attack for the day. I am coming Elizabeth, I will be there soon if they keep this up.

It was the unknown number again, I answered yes, how may I help you? She said I forgot to tell you I will need a check for $100,000 when I arrive.

I stuttered as I asked, O-N-E hundred thousand American dollars, is that correct?

She said yes Lamb Skin, have my money ready when I get there.

Reverend Allen, I too thought, this can't be real. Someone is playing a sick joke on a very sick woman.

I started thinking what if this was God and I

miss him if I don't do what this woman says. Listen as I tell you the real truth. A peace settled on me like, a blanket covering you on a cold winters night.

In that peace I began to pray and for two days I found myself locked in the sanctuary. For the first time in two days my phone rang. Guess who was calling? Yes, it was Sister Faith. Before I could say hello she began dishing out orders.

I am on my way and I need you to call someone you trust with your spiritual life. Have them to come to you right now. I will be there shortly after they arrive. With those words she hung up in my ear again. I thought it was just me but she hung up on Rev too and the sound of the laughter that I am getting from the crowd, she must have hung up on y'all too.

I immediately called Evangelist Grant. I told her to meet me at the church right now. In less than ten minutes she was banging on the sanctuary doors. After unlocking the doors and disarming the alarm, I let her in and said, sit down and don't ask me anything. We will get all our questions answered shortly.

We sat there saying absolutely nothing for two hours. Going into the third hour I broke the silence.

I am sorry Grant for dragging you down here for nothing. Before she could form a reply, Sister Faith walked in the sanctuary.

As I watched this little lady walk towards me I felt a strong and powerful presence moving with her. It was like standing in the open during a silent, and violent lightning storm. She had my full attention.

Good evening ladies, we have no time to waste, I am Sister Faith we will get the warm and fuzzies later right now the clock is ticking. She looked at me and said, Kitty-Pup it is going to be just fine. God is unable to make mistakes. One day y'all special-ed preachers are gonna realize who's service you enlisted in.

I don't know what she was thinking, but Grant interrupted Sister Faith's speech and said, I am Evangelist Grant how may I help you ma'am?

Sister Faith looked at her and said, first of all if you could help I wouldn't be here right now. I am gonna need you to sit your hips down someplace and pray like people are gonna die if you don't. Now Miss Helper let me see you get that right.

Sister Faith rolled her eyes and turned her

attention back to me. You better believe Grant went to a corner like she was put in time-out and she prayed louder than I ever heard her pray before. Without turning back in her direction Sister Faith yelled out, the Lord can hear very well, you don't need to holler at him Flower-Bug. I gave you the benefit of the doubt that you would get this right. Now before you start over and do it right, pray that the Lord help you with your pride and ego issues we can see it and it's not cute, Miss Sister Evangelist Grant.

She began to spit out orders to me again. Call your husband and tell him you will be in a prayer shut in at church for the next two days. Tell him to pack you an overnight bag and leave it by the front door for Grant to grab later tonight.

I did exactly what I was told. I hadn't spoken to my husband since my second day in the hospital. The only question he had, was what time Grant was coming by for the bag. I was about to lay into him when Sister Faith took my phone and hung it up. I remember thinking it would have felt better if she had let me hang up on him.

"Come sit down and let me tell you a story Sweet Plum." The names she use to call people were hilarious, she had a thing for fruit and animals.

She has called me everything from Strawberry Nugget to Apple Kitty.

The crowd erupted in laughter as everyone started to remember all the names from Sister Faith.

She began her story like this: "I have seen situations much worse than this Sweet-Pea." God is able to rewrite any story in this life. When he puts his spin on a situation, Honey-Buns tragedy looks like advantage, sickness looks like health, humiliation looks like respect, shame looks like honor, and death looks like life.

When you serve the Lord of Lords there is absolutely no lost. Lost looks like gain. Do you understand what I am telling you Dumpling?

If I can be honest Ms. Faith, I hear you, I actually believe all you have spoken. I'm not surprised by the ability of the Lord to change everything in a split second. I just don't see how I look on the other side of the change.

Here is a problem with you big time preachers, you all go through that one big issue that you think will end your world, you turn to the Lord, you serve him with passion and excitement. After a while of seeing him work through you, you get comfortable and forget that in the mist of your service and all the celebrations of victory and the blessings that are showered down from on high, there is an adversary lurking, learning and full of patience. He sits back and waits for the perfect opportunity to show up in your life again.

He lets you win those little battles, to weaken you for the time of war. But you can't tell y'all Rock-Head preachers nothing until you on the ground. If you go to a service to get something like you use too, you would have seen it coming. But y'all attend services like you are the special guest, critiquing the speakers you think are unsubstantial to you. Today your eyes are open and you are ready for orders. Didn't you know every service you attended gave orders for today? You couldn't have known or else you would have been prepared for this season.

Have you ever watched the water on a lake? If you watch it closely enough it will speak to you. The waters teaches a lesson that we are too busy to learn. On a clear day the water is still and calm, in a resting position. When the wind is blowing, the water picks up a steady pace and flows with it. If a storm is raging the water goes roughly with the currents.

Todays servants run life like this. When there is a calm they run full force into a bright idea. By the time the wind picks up you block-heads are getting tired and still trying to provide holy service to the Lord's people. By the time the storm hits you are too tired to fight and you drown time and time again. Good thing the Lord shows us mercy. If he didn't we would all be fish food.

Step 1 - When your life is in a resting season Baby-Gum, rest.

Step 2 - When it is time to work you will have to pick up the pace and move with the spirit.

Step 3 - When the storm hits you have sustained enough momentum to roll with the tides. Roll on!

Step 4 - Live a little then repeat as often as necessary.

If you truly are in tune with the Lord, life will most certainly happen to and around you. Real life will show up live and in living color to your door. Just remember the seasons don't show up in order, you have to always be aware of the signs and your instructions.

Now, enough of that, I have learned the hard

way to stay on task, when you off track everything lasts longer.

Sister Faith had a way with words. She took the simple things in life to say a major message. Now as I end my Sister Faith story I want every one of you to know, It's about to sound crazy. If I wasn't there every step of the way I would never believe this story coming from someone else.

I fell asleep and when I opened my eyes the sun was shining bright through the window of my office. I jumped up and said we never got my bag from the house. Sister Faith laughed and said, "Block-Head Preachers are hilarious".

I didn't know if I should ask what she meant or punch her little old behind in the mouth. I know I am a minister and this was an old lady, but the honesty in my life is not afraid to say, "I wanted to slap this $100K old lady in her smart mouth." As all of you who have encountered her, you know I shut my mouth and let her continue.

Now Love-Bug I am going to need you to go wash your face and do something with that breath. Sister Evangelist, you are up. I need you to get your messiest member and at six this evening I want y'all to go pick up the overnight bag by the front door of the house. Can I trust you with that?

Evangelist Grant looked like she was afraid to respond and just shook her head and sat in silence.

Sister Faith continued with her instructions. When you get to the house use the key to open the door, grab the bag and return here immediately.

While she is doing that you and I will celebrate your exodus from this mess you made of your life.

I asked angrily, "What do you mean the mess I made, you don't even know what happened and how this mess came about". I had no control over this outcome.

"You had control!" she yelled out and scared the crap out of me. The Lord wants to keep me in near stroke mode. I guess I deserved it for the thoughts I was having. I sat holding my heart as she brought the knives out and commenced to carving a sculpture of what I thought was a good life.

I get tired of you church folks, you get married for style and you don't wait for the mate the Lord prescribed for you. I know all I need to know about your situation. You got married to a man who used your gifts to his advantage. He was never faithful to you and you knew it. Now you are in this situation and you are more concerned about what people will think than you are concerned with what the Lord is doing. Have I just about summed it up for you?

I dropped my head in shame because she was absolutely correct about everything. I married him because he was fine and I needed arm candy for church. From day one he was more trouble than I ever imagined I could participate in. I knew he had relationships with other women and he used my clout and contacts to build him a world of privilege.

My dad said please don't do this, you can wait on the Lord. I tried to explain to my dad that I was a young minister ready to go out a preach the gospel to the world. The part he didn't understand was, in order for me to be allowed to work in ministry they said, I had to be married and he was willing and available.

Love-Buns, you don't have to be anything but willing to work in the service of the Lord. Your heart was all for the Lord but your mind was still stuck in religion. It is when we totally commit ourselves to the Lord that we receive the ability to operate in his full power. Not because we do things, but because he is and will always be in control.

I think my work here is just about done. Nothing should surprise you after this ordeal is behind you. God will change everything to work out for his good and you will reap the benefits, if you stand in the proper position. Now, I am gonna need my check before you get all caught up in the spirit and forget.

I could not believe that in the mist of ministering to me this woman asked about money. I forgot about everything that was happening in my life since she has been here but tomorrow is still coming and I don't see her way as being the best way for me. I certainly didn't see $100K worth of anything being done.

Sister Faith laughed out loud and said, "You can never pay for anything the Lord does. His works are priceless. So if your mind is on a $100K cure, you will be sick until your funds run out and you die. The money is a seed, that will grow where planted. She laughed again like she was tickled by her own words and how did she know what I was thinking?

We have a healing service scheduled for 7pm tonight, can you lead the service Sister Faith? I don't think I have it in me to touch anyone today.

You are gonna have a healing service, too bad I

won't be here to witness it. My job is done here. I will be in touch soon. You are everything the Lord needs you to be. He will never leave his own to defend themselves. The battles are yours, and mostly self inflicted. When war rages know those are his fights and no matter how bad you want to jump in, the Lord don't need your help. The Lord is Good and you are what ever you want to be.

She spoke those words as she gathered her things and walked right out the way she walked in. I was so confused and I had no idea what I was supposed to do.

Evangelist Grant and Sister Thelma were off to get my bag from the house and I prepared the church for the service. My mind was all over the place trying to figure out my next moves.

It was 5:45 and the congregation began to fill the sanctuary for the healing service. I was nervous because Evangelist had not come back to the church yet.

At 6:15 I decided to begin. I allowed one of the ministers to lead the service because I was no good for anything. The praise team started to sing. I called Evangelist Grant to see what was taking them so long. Ten calls and I didn't get one answer. I said a quick prayer and went to the sanctuary.

It was a packed house for an evening service, I thought maybe I should be officiating this service myself, but I felt peace and it said...rest!

I remembered not to interfere with the Lord's work. Minister Greene did a wonderful job of leading the service until he did the unthinkable. He opened the floor for people to speak. We have always had a problem with this in our ministry.

When you give people the microphone, they never know what to say or when to stop talking so we don't really do that in our ministry. When he did it a few of the mothers got up to say how good the Lord had been to them. Some people prayed for the sick and shut in, while others complained about everything from dry chicken to wet toilet paper.

I thought to myself after the next person I am going to wrap this up and close with a group prayer. The last young lady to get to the microphone was an unfamiliar face. I had never seen her in our church before. As she reached Minister Greene, he asked if she was okay. She was frail and looked to be about eighteen. She looked like she was once a beautiful girl, but something had drained the life out of her.

As she reached for the microphone, everyone in attendance including me were all ears. We were waiting to hear what this young lady had to say.

Hello, my name is Jessica. I have never been a church goer or anything like that, but I do remember going to church with my grandma when I was small and her telling me when my back is against the wall call on the Lord and he will come through. I also remember them saying to confess your sins to be saved. I came here tonight to confess my sins. When I was thirteen I met a twenty-five year old man. We had a relationship for four years before I found out I was HIV positive and pregnant with his son.

When I told my man-friend about everything, he denied me, my illness and my child. I came here today to say I am sorry. I knew right from wrong and I chose wrong. The doctors say they have done all they can for me. I don't have family and I don't want my baby to grow up in foster care.

He didn't contract HIV or the virus, the Lord protected him from my mistakes and I am grateful. He is at the Lasting Love Daycare Center and I left a message that he would be picked up by Helen Stackhouse this evening.

I was already in deep thought with her every word touching some parts of my life, but when she said my name I lost my breath and had to sit down for a second. Members rushed over to me to see if I was okay.

While I was given water and towels, I didn't notice the commotion on the floor. The young lady fainted right there in the sanctuary. When the ambulance arrived they worked on her and they rushed her to the emergency room. I had Minister Greene go with them to the hospital, while I went to see about her baby boy.

As I was driving to the Daycare I could not believe all that was happening in such a short time. When I arrived I showed my identification and the woman at the front desk asked me to step into the conference room. All I was thinking is what am I getting into now.

A man and woman came into the room and closed the door behind them. I was nervous to say the least, but I waited for them to start talking.

Hello Mrs. Stackhouse the man said as he shook my hand and took a seat, this is Ms. Hall our case worker. We greeted each other as she took a seat beside me.

As you know Timothy's mother is really sick and she has you down as her emergency contact.

I interrupted him and said, emergency contact I don't even know his mother. I just laid eyes on her for the first time about an hour ago. How could I be her emergency contact? I search my mind to see if I ministered to her at some point but everything came up blank.

The caseworker interrupted my thoughts by saying, I have all the adoption paperwork here for you to sign tonight. Jessica, his mom has signed all parental rights over to you. You can take Timothy tonight and raise him as your own.

A baby? How can I raise a baby in my state, do they have a clue of what I am dealing with in my own life? I asked, if I don't take him what will happen to him?

The man said, he will become a ward of the state and placed in foster care until we can find him a home.

As the tears ran down my face I explained that I was a ward of the state until I was fifteen. After years of horrible foster parents, I was blessed with a couple who loved each other and loved me. I could not let this baby go through foster care. I excused myself and went to the restroom.

Lord what is happening? What will I do with a baby? Then my phone rang, it was Minister Greene. He said that Jessica didn't make it and I needed to get back to the church immediately. Lord, what else could possibly be happening now?

Without thinking a second thought I went back to the room and signed every paper the social worker had in her file. I asked if I could get the baby, because I had to get back to church, I left in the middle of a service.

They brought little Timothy to me and he was the cutest thing I had ever seen. The social worker gave me copies of all paperwork and an envelope. I gathered the few things he had, strapped him in his car seat and headed back to church.

There was an accident about ten cars ahead of me. As we sat in traffic I began to look over the files and I open the envelope the social worker gave me. In it was a note that read:

Dear Ms. Helen

I am sorry for being in a relationship with your husband. I hope you can love Timothy the way his parents never could. You never have to tell him about either of us.

Jessica

It was a silent drive back, I was in a daze and I looked back to see little Timothy smiling at me with those big precious and innocent eyes. Well, its you and me kid, is what I said as I pulled into the parking lot of the church.

There was so much activity at the front of the church, cars were double parked and people were yelling. As I got closer Evangelist Grant ran over to me before I could find out what was happening.

Franticly she began to explain, We went to your house to get your bag. When we pulled into the driveway we heard people yelling so we ran to see what was happening. Three woman had your husband tied to a chair and was yelling how he destroyed their lives.

He admitted to having relationships with each of them and he apologized for giving them HIV.

When he saw me he said to tell you he was sorry

and he will be gone by the time you get home and you will never see him again. I thought this was a joke but Sister Thelma recorded the whole incident and has posted it to social media. Now the entire ministry is in an uproar about how foul he is for doing you like that.

I walked up to the building with my new baby on my hip and put order back to the house. Everyone was so loving to me and little Timothy.

All I can say is the Lord does what he does the way he does it and that is forever good enough for me. I know the truth of the scripture that reads: Genesis 50:20 As for you, you meant evil against me, but God meant it for good… Today I stand before you twenty-five years later healthy and blessed. I have a twenty-six year old son, who is practicing law and a ministry full of people who genuinely love the Lord. No matter what situation you find your self in, be it self inflicted or just one of those things that happen. The Lord takes care of his people period.

And about that laugh that everyone is talking about. Today I too understand that God kind of humor.

As I take my seat let me tell you how funny the

Lord can be. Ten years after that crazy day, guess who walked into my new church, in a new state, on the first day of services? None other than my ex-husband and his new wife.

He explained he had been living in the area since he left. He apologized for everything that he has done. Then explained how he is truly saved and married a woman who was already HIV positive. From that day, we both co-parented (our) son. His wife who could never give birth had the opportunity to be a co-mom. The Lord is hilarious, thanks Sister Faith for your servant life. We will always love you.

Closing Remarks & Prayers

Today we have heard some life changing stories about Sister Faith. But I am still wondering how old she really was? The crowd erupted in laughter and chatter. Now that I am aware this stadium is filled with preachers I will keep it clean, sorry for my choice of words earlier.

I have been sitting here trying to calculate how old she really was. If she started her ministry when she was well over eighty, and spent three days with each of the hundred-thousand ministries represented here today, not to mention the ones outside, let's do the math.

She spent 3 days with 100,000 ministries, that would take 300,000 days. 300,000 days is about 821 years. If she started her real ministry well over the age of 80, she would have to have been over 901 years old. That can't be right, she looked like a sassy seventy year old. No one lives that long anymore. But I believe if we live right we will be able to ask the Lord for ourselves one day. Today Sister Faith and her age will remain a mystery.

After hearing all the events that took place with

the few speakers today, I would say this woman was sent straight from heaven to show us how the Lord really works.

Not just her name but her as a person is evidence that we are involved in something much bigger than we are imagining.

By profession I am a teacher, I have been teaching middle school children for ten years. I have taught a lesson and experienced failures and successes during testing. Sister Faith said be me, so I have to give a lecture type sermon today and I am confident some will understand and others will need further assistance and believe me that is perfectly okay, because we all learn at different levels and in different ways.

Let me tell you a story that was shared with me by one of the students from my first year of teaching, shared after she graduated from high school.

Her name was Ruth Naomi, when I met her she was a very insecure young lady. She always wanted to answer every question correctly and worked hard to get all A's in class. I never knew what drove this little girl to want to be the best of everything she did.

When I heard her speak at a church function I was floored to find out the reasons she pushed so hard. She started her story by telling that she was born third in a family of six children. When she was six her parents separated for reasons she was never aware of. All she knew was that her family life had changed drastically.

She watched her mother work harder than ever to keep them fed and clothed. Her older siblings would work around the house to help her mother with the younger kids. Ruth thought at a young age that if she had done better in school and cleaned her room everyday maybe her parents would still be together.

She took the responsibility for her parents failed marriage all on her shoulders and that made her determined to do everything right. She got the best grades in school and that made her mom happy, she always received awards and high praises from others and her mother would seem to appreciate the complements.

Then she shared the pit falls that grew with her living this type of life. She said at the end of every season in her life she always ended up empty and hurt. No matter what she did to please people she felt pain and it was exhausting.

When she accepted the Lord as her own personal savior, she realized she was more than enough. Her efforts to please people were for nothing, her life was meant to please the Lord and him alone.

It was a difficult transition from being the poster child for perfection and just being okay being Ruth, the one the Lord loves and wants to use for his purposes.

She is now one of the greatest teachers of phycology and she shares her story so people can realize its not how you start. It is the process you take to finish.

Now let me teach someone something today. Enculturation is the method that we learn to function in a particular culture. We learn our values, what is considered normal and our world views from observation, experience and instruction. We learn to adapt qualities that are appropriate and necessary to be successful within our community and or culture. We learn these lessons from our parents, peers and teachers.

When making the transition from just existing to

becoming a child of the Lord, we have to start the enculturation process all over again. That's why we attend church and listen to the messages from the teachers, so that we can gain a new worldview and live out a different type of normalcy.

We sometimes get so excited by the new us that we have become we forget that the people we deal with closely have come from a different upbringing than we did. We forget that there are processes to everything but we expect others to be perfect saints and we try our hardest to be perfect before others.

I don't know all the answers but I have many questions on the topic of living for the Lord. Today I have heard ministries deal with lust, greed, pride, insecurities and even suicide.

It seems like we get distracted with self: who we are and how we are perceived by others. We become dissatisfied with the Lord: when our lives don't match completely with what we think it should be.

That causes us to need justification from others: approval that what we are doing is pleasing to everyone else. Then we vindicate our situations by justification in the works we do. Now I am no bible scholar but it looks like we miss the mark along the way. If we take the life of Sister Faith as yet another example the Lord sent our way. We should know that no matter where you come from, no matter what you have done with your life to this point. The Lord thinks you are more than enough. You were made for an assignment that only you can accomplish.

There are convictions in your life that no one can change. We will be effective line-leaders when we learn the culture of the Lord. Keep praying, keep fasting keep doing what ever you feel necessary to keep the line moving in the direction of the Lord.

We were perfectly created but we are not meant to be perfect beings. The Lord's perfection is the process of becoming not the achievement of getting there first.

I will close her party with this:

Now faith is the assurance of things hoped for, the conviction of things not seen. For by it the people of old received their commendation. By faith we understand that the universe was created by the word of God, so that what is seen was not made out of things that are visible. **Hebrews 11:1-3**

She was living proof that the Lord is real and active in our everyday lives. The effects of her ministry are forever evidence to each of us that we are all a part of a bigger plan. To honor her life and legacy I challenge each person represented here today to go out and spend three days with ten people and prove your FAITH IS REAL!

Thank you for purchasing Sister Faith's Diaries Volume One. These volumes can be given as gifts, used to spark discussion at various personal ministry and family functions.

If you enjoyed the story and the messages that were shared, please continue to support this ministry by purchasing copies of upcoming Sister Faith's Diaries Volumes.

Coming Soon

Volume 2
Help! Your Church is Too Confusing

Volume 3
Synthetic Oil

Volume 4
Two Become One…When It's Convenient

Volume 5
I'll Walk

Volume 6
Can My House Stand the Storm

Volume 7
Little Christians

Volume 8
Imperfect Imperfections

Volume 9
Who In the Hell Are You

Volume 10
Shifting, But Stuck in Neutral

Volume 11

Who's Your Daddy

Volume 12
Hustlers Hoes and Pimps

Volume 13
Trap House Church

Volume 14
Camouflaged Pride

World News

Today a World News reporter attended the funeral services of Faith Christian.

Ms. Christian passed on October 13, 2018 of natural causes at her home in the Big City.

Saints University Christain Academy's entire campus was recently renovated. It is unconfirmed but our sources believe Ms. Christian was solely financially responsible for the renovations. It has been reported over 100K preachers from all over the world attended the services of this phenomenal woman.

Also further reports state, over 10K people gathered outside of the stadium and watched the service on large monitors placed around the campus.

Sister Faith as she was known to many left a few other surprises to her friends.

After renovation, Ms. Christian purchased the grounds and building the college owned and renamed the location to the Faith Full Christian Center.

The school was relocated 3 miles south of its original site in a new state of the art campus built just to say thank you.

She was a generous woman and we look forward to reporting more

about her life and the legacy she left behind.

Let's Talk

Are you saved? _____

If no, why not?

_____

_____

_____

If yes, how do you know you are saved?

_____

_____

_____

Is God real? _____

How did you come to form your answer?

_____

_____

_____

Can you be a line-leader to heaven? _____

If no, why not?

_____

_____

_____

If yes, how can you lead your line?

_____

_____

_____

List three points made in the story that touched you and why:

1. _____
2. _____
3. _____